D1444581

Snow White

NOTE TO PARENTS

Based on the beloved Walt Disney motion picture *Snow White and the Seven Dwarfs,* this book focuses on what happens when Snow White finds herself lost and alone in the forest. Seeing her fright, the kind woodland creatures understand that Snow White is unable to find her way to safety by herself. They help by leading Snow White to a cottage where she can find shelter.

The cottage is a mess inside, and Snow White realizes that the absent owners cannot keep house for themselves. She decides to help by cleaning their house and cooking a hot supper. When the owners—the Seven Dwarfs—return home and hear Snow White's story, they know they must help her. They learn what Snow White has learned—it is right to help others when they cannot help themselves.

This book recounts one memorable episode from the movie that will help children learn an important lesson about the value of helping. For the complete story of *Snow White and the Seven Dwarfs,* look for these other Golden Books:

Walt Disney's
Snow White
Finds a Home
A BOOK ABOUT HELPING

A GOLDEN BOOK • NEW YORK
Western Publishing Company, Inc., Racine, Wisconsin 53404

©1987 The Walt Disney Company. All rights reserved. Printed in the U.S.A. by Western Publishing Company, Inc.
No part of this book may be reproduced or copied in any form without written permission from the copyright owner.
GOLDEN®, GOLDEN & DESIGN®, and A GOLDEN BOOK® are trademarks of Western Publishing Company, Inc.
Library of Congress Catalog Card Number: 86-72416   ISBN: 0-307-11671-9 / ISBN: 0-307-61671-1 (lib. bdg.)
A B C D E F G H I J K L M

Once upon a time there lived a Princess named Snow White. Everyone loved her, for she was kind and good. Everyone, that is, but her stepmother, the Queen!

The Queen was vain and jealous. She hated Snow White just because the Princess was pretty. She made Snow White wear shabby clothes, and she ordered her to scrub and sweep like a servant.

Snow White didn't mind working, but she knew her stepmother hated her, and she was afraid.

One day the Queen's huntsman took Snow White out to walk in the forest near the castle. For a little while she was happy.

"It's nice here in the woods," she said to the huntsman. "It's so peaceful. While I'm here the Queen can't see me or hurt me."

Then the huntsman spoke up. "You must go away," he said. "Hide from the Queen, for she means to harm you.

"Now run away, quickly!"

Snow White ran deep into the forest. Soon she came to a rushing river, and there was no way to get across.

"Oh, dear!" said Snow White. "I must find shelter. Oh, where can I go? I'm so frightened!"

She fell to the ground and began to cry.

The birds heard Snow White crying and came to land on the trees above her. They watched the Princess, and they waited.

Animals came from their hiding places in the woods. Squirrels scampered down from the treetops. Rabbits crept out of their burrows. Even the slow, steady turtle left his pond and came to see the weeping Princess.

After a while, Snow White stopped crying. She sat up,
and the animals came closer. They chirped and chattered,
and nudged at her arm.

Suddenly Snow White was not afraid anymore. "You're
trying to help me, aren't you?" she said to the animals.

She stood up, and the animals tugged at her skirt. They led her down a path to a clearing in the woods.

Snow White saw a little cottage in the clearing. "Perhaps the people who live in that cottage can help me," said Snow White.

She knocked at the door. When no one answered, she looked in through a window.

She saw a dusty table and seven dusty little chairs inside the cottage. There were dirty dishes in the sink. There were cobwebs in the corners and crumpled clothes on the floor.

"Little children must live in this house," said Snow White. "*Untidy* little children! Poor things! They surely need help.

"Perhaps *I* can help them," said Snow White. "I'll clean the house and wash the dishes. Then I'll cook something good, and when the children come home, they can have a nice hot supper!"

Snow White opened the door and walked into the cottage.

She found a broom and set to work. The animals helped
her. A rabbit held the dustpan while she swept. A squirrel
used his tail to brush the cobwebs from the corners. The
chipmunks dusted the table. The badger picked up the
soiled clothes.

After the house was clean, Snow White made a big kettle
of soup. She put all sorts of good things in it.
Soon the soup was bubbling on the hearth.

Snow White went up the stairs to the loft, where seven little beds stood in a row. The beds looked soft and inviting.

Snow White yawned. "I'm so tired," she said. "I think I'll take a nap." She stretched out across three of the beds and closed her eyes. In no time, she was fast asleep.

While she slept the sun went down. The woods grew
dark, and seven little men came marching toward the
cottage.

The little men were the Seven Dwarfs, who lived in the
cottage. They had been working all day in their diamond
mine, and now they were tired and hungry.

As they came into the clearing they saw their cottage.
"Look!" shouted one of the dwarfs. "A light! Someone's in
our house!"

"Careful, men," warned Doc, who was the leader of the
dwarfs. "We'd better sneak up on him—or it!"

Doc led the way into the cottage. The other dwarfs
tiptoed behind him.

He lifted the latch. Carefully he pushed open the door.
The dwarfs peeked in. And what did they see?
They saw a fire making a cheery glow. They saw a kettle
on the fire, bubbling and steaming as if it held something
very tasty.

"Someone's cooked supper for us!" cried the dwarf named Happy.

"And swept the floor!" Sneezy said with a sneeze.

"And wiped away the cobwebs," Sleepy said, yawning.

"Someone's dusted the chairs," whispered Bashful.

Grumpy scowled. "Goblins!" he said. "Or witches! They did all this so's they could catch us off guard! It's what witches and goblins do. I'll bet they're hiding now, waiting to jump out and grab us!"

"Courage, men!" cried Doc. "We're going to find them, whatever they are!"

The dwarfs began to search. Sleepy looked behind the door. Bashful peeked into the woodbox. Sneezy held his candle high and peered down into the cellar.

At last, holding on to each other, the dwarfs crept up the stairs to the loft. And what did they find? Not a witch or a goblin. They found a pretty girl, taking a nap on their beds!

Snow White awoke when the dwarfs came in. She sat up and told the little men how she had found her way to their cottage. "The animals helped me," she said. "They brought me here. I can't go back to the castle because I'm afraid of my stepmother, the Queen."

"The Queen?" said Doc. "You should be afraid of her. She's a witch!"

The dwarfs decided on the spot that they would help the Princess. They would let her stay with them, and they would keep her safe.

"Oh, thank you all for helping me," Snow White cried. Dopey looked puzzled. "Don't you know what helping is?" Snow White said.

"Helping is doing something nice for someone—something nice that person can't do for herself. You've all done something very nice for me—and I'm so glad I could do something nice for you." And she led them down to supper.

Snow White's soup was the tastiest meal the dwarfs had eaten in many a long day. That night there was dancing and merriment in the little cottage. The forest animals peeked through the windows to share in the fun. They felt happy, too—they had helped Snow White find a home with the Seven Dwarfs.